Amazing
ANIMAL FAMILIES

Tick Tock Direct

With thanks to: Sally Morgan, Trudi Webb, Jean Coppendale, and Elizabeth Wiggans

North American edition copyright © ticktock Entertainment Ltd. 2010

First published in North America in 2010 by ticktock
The Pantiles Chambers, 85 High Street, Tunbridge Wells, Kent TN1 1XP

ISBN 978-1-84696-203-5

Printed in China
9 8 7 6 5 4 3 2

Picture credits (t=top; b=bottom; c=center; l=left; r=right; OFC=outside front cover; OBC=outside back cover):
Ardea: 26c. Wendy Blanshard, Australian Koala Foundation, www.savethekoala.com: 24t. Corbis: 18 main, 19t, 29t, 34c, 42tl, 44c. FLPA: 8t, 11 main, 13tl, 14tl, 14c, 19b, 22c, 24 main, 39cl, 39tl, 41t, 41r, 43b, 46b, 47t, 47b, 51cl, 52b, 57b, 58b, 62, 63, 66, 67, 69t, 72b, 73t, 74b, 75b, 79b, 82c, 89t, 89c, 90–91 (all). Thomas Dressler/ardea.com: OFC. iStock: 5b, OBCtc, OBC br.
Nature Picture Library: 9t, 14–15 main, 48, 49, 61cr, 61cl, 83t, 87tr. NHPA: 28b, 44c, 60cl, 65b, 93t.Oxford Scientific Photo Library: 15t, 16c. Shutterstock: 1, 2, 4 (all), 5t, 6–7, 8tl, 8tr, 9b, 10t, 10 main, 11t, 12 (all), 12–13c, 13tr, 13cr, 13b, 18tl, 20tl, 21t, 21 main, 22tl, 22–23 main, 23t, 24tl, 25t, 25b, 26tl, 27b, 28tl, 29 main, 30–31, 32tl, 32–33 main, 32b, 33t, 34tl, 35t, 35b, 36 (all), 37, 38 (all), 38–39c, 39cr, 39b, 40tl, 44tl, 45, 46tl, 50 (all), 51r, 52tl, 53 (all), 54–55, 56tl, 56c, 57t, 58tl, 59t, 59b, 60ct, 60cr, 60b, 61b, 61t, 64 main, 65t, 68tl, 68b, 69b, 70–71, 74t, 76tl, 76b, 77, 78, 80–81 (all), 84 (all), 86–87, 88tl, 88–89b, 92tl, 93b, OBC tr, OBC bl.
Superstock: 8bl, 16tl, 16–17 main, 22b, 28c, 33b, 42b, 43t, 73b, 76c, 79t, 82tl, 83b, 85t, 85b, 92b.
ticktock Media Archive: 44 (globe), 64tl, 72tl, 75t

Every effort has been made to trace copyright holders, and we apologize in advance for any omissions.
We would be pleased to insert the appropriate acknowledgments in any subsequent edition of this publication.

Contents

Words that look
bold like this are
in the glossary.

Introduction

Animal families come in all shapes and sizes. Meet the different types of animal families—**mammals**, birds, fish, **reptiles**, and **amphibians**—and discover some amazing animal facts!

This feathery parrot is a bird.

A zebra is a mammal. Zebra babies are called foals. Zebras are pregnant for around 12–14 months.

Sea horses are fish. Baby sea horses are called fry. Sea horses are pregnant for between 14 days and four weeks.

AMAZING ANIMAL LIFE CYCLES
A life cycle is all the different **stages** and changes that a plant or animal goes through during its life.

Frogs are amphibians. Frogs lay spawn that develop into tadpoles after two weeks. The tadpoles then grow into baby frogs that are called froglets.

Flamingos are birds. Baby flamingos are called chicks. Once the eggs have been laid, it takes around one month for the chicks to **hatch**.

Mammal Families

What is a mammal?

A mammal is an animal that feeds its babies milk. Mammals are **endothermic**. This means their body **temperature** stays the same no matter how hot or cold the air or water is around them.

This Highland cow is a mammal.

Most mammals give birth to live babies. When a baby mammal is born, the mother feeds it milk from inside her body. This is called **suckling**.

A hairy hippo nose!

Mammals also have hair on their bodies. A hippopotamus is a mammal with smooth skin, but it has hair in its ears and on its nose.

The leopard cubs in this picture are suckling from their mother.

8

This pipistrelle bat is sitting on a scientist's finger while he studies it.

Mammals can be tiny like a pipistrelle bat or enormous like an elephant!

Did you know that people are mammals, too?

Mom meets Dad

Some mammals **mate**, and then the male and female bring up their young together. Other mammals meet, mate, and then the female is left to care for the babies alone or with other females in a group.

Koala dads don't help take care of their babies.

A male and a female meerkat become a couple. They lead a family group and are the only ones in the group that are allowed to have babies.

AMAZING MAMMAL FACT
Meerkats live in big family groups of around 40 animals.

When a male and female wart hog have mated, the male leaves. Adult male wart hogs live on their own.

Male wart hogs fight over who gets to mate with a female.

When a male killer whale is grown up and ready to mate, he goes to another pod and mates with a female. Then he swims back to live with his mother in his family group. Female orcas bring up their babies in their family group.

The killer whale couple swims around each other—it's like dancing!

Amazing mammal life cycles

In this section, we will find out about some amazing mammal life cycles—from killer whales who live in the ocean to treetop koalas.

A koala

A killer whale

2

A female mammal gives birth to a live baby or babies.

1

This is the life cycle of a lion.

When they become adults, male and female mammals meet and mate.

6

Some mammals live with their family group when they grow up. Others go off and live on their own.

3

Female mammals feed their babies milk.

4

Lions are meat eaters.

Mammal mothers care for their babies. Sometimes the fathers help, too.

5

Mammals teach their babies how to hunt, or find food. Young meat eaters practice their hunting skills on one another.

Pipistrelle bats

Pipistrelle bats usually have one baby each year. Hundreds of female bats gather together to give birth in a building such as a church or a barn. Sometimes they gather under a bridge or in a cave.

Father bats do not help care for the babies.

Bat pup

Mother bat

A baby bat is called a pup. When the pups are born, the mothers and pups stay together in a huge group called a nursery roost.

LIFE CYCLE FACT

A pipistrelle bat is pregnant for around 50 days. A female starts to have babies when she is between six and 12 months old.

A newborn pup clings to its mother's fur if she needs to carry it from place to place.

A mother bat can find her own pup among hundreds of other bats. She knows its smell and sound.

This pup is suckling from its mother.

Pups can fly by themselves when they are between two and four weeks old. They leave their mothers when they are eight weeks old.

This picture shows bats in a nursery roost.

Giant anteaters

Giant anteaters live on hot, dry **grasslands** in South America. Adult giant anteaters live alone. When a male and female have mated, the male leaves.

An anteater's claws grow to 4 in. (10cm) long.

The female giant anteater gives birth standing up on her back legs.

An anteater can use its tail for support, like a third leg.

AMAZING MAMMAL FACT

A baby anteater is born with fur and sharp claws. It crawls onto its mother's back, where she licks it clean. Baby anteaters suckle for around six months.

After a few months, the baby hops off its mother's back to explore and then hops on again.

The baby stays with its mother until it is grown up, around the age of two.

If the baby falls off, it grunts to let its mother know.

Killer whales

Killer whale babies, called calves, are born under the water, tail first. A killer whale calf can be 8 ft. (2.5m) long when it is born! Killer whales are also called orcas.

A newborn killer whale weighs 400 lbs. (180kg).

LIFE CYCLE FACT

Killer whales are pregnant for 15–18 months. Females start to have babies when they are around 15 years old.

As soon as the calf is born, the mother pushes the baby to the surface so that it can take its first breath of air.

The mother killer whale guides the calf to the surface of the water using her flippers and nose.

Calf

Flipper

A killer whale calf feeds on its mother's milk for the first one or two years of its life.

the mother whale teaches the calf how to hunt and catch food.

Most killer whale pods have around 30 members.

Killer whale families talk to one another using grunts, whistles, and squeals. Calves learn how to make these noises.

Meerkats

Meerkats live in groups, called kits, that include males, females, and babies. They live in **burrows** under the ground.

A meerkat's dark eye rings protect its eyes from the bright sun.

LIFE CYCLE FACT

Meerkats are pregnant for 75 days. A female starts to have babies when she is one year old.

Newborn kits are helpless and do not have hair. They are born in a burrow and stay there until they are around three or four weeks old.

Female meerkats have three to five babies at one time.

Adult meerkats take turns baby-sitting while others go out hunting.

Meerkats stand up on their back legs to keep watch for predators such as eagles.

When the kits are around one month old, they start to go on hunting trips. Each kit has its own adult that teaches it how to hunt.

Wart hogs

A female wart hog gives birth to two or three babies at one time in an underground burrow. The babies, or piglets, leave the burrow when they are around two weeks old.

Wart hogs use their good sense of smell to find food.

It is important that the newborn piglets do not get wet or cold. They sleep on a raised shelf at the back of the burrow to make sure they stay dry.

Adult wart hogs and older piglets enjoy a mud bath to cool off on a hot day.

Wart hogs use their sharp **tusks** to fight off predators such as lions. Both male and female wart hogs have tusks.

Wart hog piglets are not born with tusks. The tusks grow as the piglets grow.

LIFE CYCLE FACT

Wart hogs are pregnant for six months. A female starts to have babies when she is 18 months old.

The piglets suckle for around four months. Male piglets stay with their mother for around two years. Females go off on their own when they are around 18 months old.

Hippopotamuses

Hippos live in a group called a **herd**. The herd includes one adult male, many females, and their young. When a female is ready to give birth, she looks for a soft place at the edge of a river.

Male hippos fight over females.

The hippo baby, or calf, is born in shallow water at the edge of a river. The mother quickly pushes the baby to the surface so that it can breathe.

LIFE CYCLE FACT

Hippos are pregnant for eight months. A female starts to have babies when she is nine years old.

The mother and calf move away from the herd for the first few weeks. This stops the baby from getting hurt accidently by one of the other adults.

An adult hippo can weigh 1.5 tons!

Most grown-up hippos stay in the herd where they were born. A male hippo may start his own herd when he is around 20 years old.

AMAZING MAMMAL FACT
Sometimes a hippo calf will rest on its mother's back. It will slip into the water if it gets too hot and then climb back on.

Koalas

Koalas are **marsupials**. This means that the mother has a **pouch** on her stomach where her baby lives. The pouch is like a pocket. A newborn koala is called a joey.

A female koala gives birth in eucalyptus trees.

LIFE CYCLE FACT

Koalas are pregnant for 35 days. A female starts to have babies when she is two years old.

This newborn joey is around the size of a jelly bean.

A newborn joey is tiny. It has no hair, ears, or eyes. It crawls inside its mother's pouch. In the pouch, the joey drinks its mother's milk.

he joey's fur, ars, and eyes row. The joey gets igger and bigger. When the joey is round six or seven months old, it starts o ride on its mother's back.

Joey

At around one year old, the joey leaves its mother. This is usually when the mother gives birth to another joey.

That's amazing!

A baby giraffe is called a calf.

All mammal mothers care for their babies. They feed them milk and teach them how to find food. But mammal babies begin life in many different ways.

Female polar bears go to sleep in a **den** for the winter. While they are in the den, they give birth to their babies, called cubs.

A polar bear's den is underneath the snow. Can you see the cub?

AMAZING MAMMAL FACT
Newborn polar bear cubs are about around 12 in. (30cm) long. They are blind, pink, and hairless.

The mother and cubs leave the den after four or five months, when it is spring.

AMAZING MAMMAL FACT
The duck-billed platypus is a very unusual mammal because it lays eggs!

The female platypus lays two or three grape-size eggs. The eggs hatch around 12 days later. The baby platypuses drink milk from their mother.

The giraffe is the world's tallest animal mother. The female gives birth standing up. The giraffe calf drops 6.5 ft. (2m) to the ground!

A newborn giraffe can be 6 ft. (1.8m) tall!

29

Bird Families

What is a bird?

Birds have something that no other animals have—feathers! Other animals have wings, and some animals lay eggs, but no other animals have feathers. A bird's feathers help keep it warm.

Water birds, such as ducks, have waterproof feathers.

Flying birds have stiff feathers that help them fly. They have small, soft feathers called **down** to stay warm.

Beak

Tail

Millions of years ago, **prehistoric** reptiles lived on Earth. These reptiles were the **ancestors** of birds.

Birds lay eggs like reptiles, but birds are endothermic animals, like mammals.

Scales

Birds have scales on their legs and feet, and claws like reptiles.

Flying feathers

Wing

Claws

Birds can be tiny, like the hummingbirds in this picture, or huge like an ostrich.

The ostrich is the biggest bird in the world. An adult male can be 8 ft. (2.5m) tall!

AMAZING BIRD FACT
An ostrich is too heavy to fly, but it can run fast. Its top speed is 43 mph (70km/h).

Mom meets Dad

Most birds **breed** every year, usually in the spring. Some stay together as a pair for life. Other birds find a new partner each year. Some females have chicks with more than one male in the same year.

A male and a female swan pair up for life.

Tail

Some male birds have colorful feathers to attract females. The male peacock shows off to the female peahen by spreading out his tail feathers like a fan.

Many male birds sing to attract a female to their **territory**. They defend their territory and their female by chasing away other males.

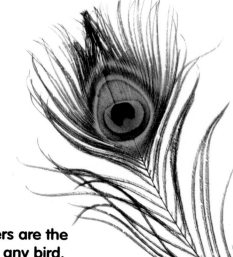

Peacock tail feathers are the longest feathers of any bird.

Some pairs of birds perform a dance together before they mate. The male blue-footed booby dances for the female. He shows her his blue feet and whistles.

The male booby spreads his wings and puts his beak up in the air as part of his dance.

AMAZING BIRD FACT
To attract a mate, the male frigate bird puffs out his bright red throat like a balloon.

Eggs and nests

Many female birds build nests on their own. Others are helped by their partner. Some birds make a nest before they mate—and some do it afterward. Then the female bird lays eggs in the nest.

This female swan is collecting leaves to put in her nest.

Some birds make nests from grass, twigs, and leaves. The flamingo makes a nest of mud with a **hollow** top.

The white stork's nest is made of sticks. The stork adds more sticks every year, so the nest gets bigger and bigger!

The female flamingo lays one or two eggs.

The female stork lays up to four eggs in her nest.

Adult woodpecker

Chick

This great spotted woodpecker makes a nest in a hole in a tree.

This bald eagle is sitting on her eggs.

Female birds sit on the eggs to keep them warm. This is called **incubation**. Some males help with this job, too, and they also bring food to the females.

Chicks hatch from the eggs. Many chicks are helpless. Mom and Dad bring food to the chicks.

In this section, we will find out about some amazing bird life cycles—from the record-breaking arctic tern to the friendly robin.

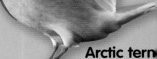

Arctic tern

A robin chick eats around 140 bugs, spiders, and worms each day!

Amazing bird life cycles

1

An adult male and female bird meet and mate.

6

This is the life cycle of a robin.

When they are ready to go off on their own, the chicks leave the nest. Some parents teach their chicks how to fly. This is a picture of a young robin.

5

The parents bring the chicks food to eat. Some birds remove their chicks' droppings from the nest, too.

2

The female lays eggs in a nest.

3

Robins live in Europe, North Africa, and parts of Asia.

4

The female sits on the eggs to keep them warm. Some male birds bring the female food while she does this.

The eggs hatch. Many newborn chicks are blind and have no feathers.

Hornbills

Hornbills live in the forests of Africa and Asia. A hornbill uses its large beak, or bill, to eat fruit and to catch insects, lizards, and snakes.

This is a southern ground hornbill. It feeds on the ground.

Most types of hornbills find their food in trees, but some feed on the ground.

This great Indian hornbill lives in trees.

LIFE CYCLE FACT
The female hornbill lays up to six eggs. The chicks hatch in around 30 or 40 days.

Hornbills nest in holes in trees. The female lays eggs and then shuts herself inside. She blocks the entrance with a wall made from droppings mixed with mud and squashed fruit.

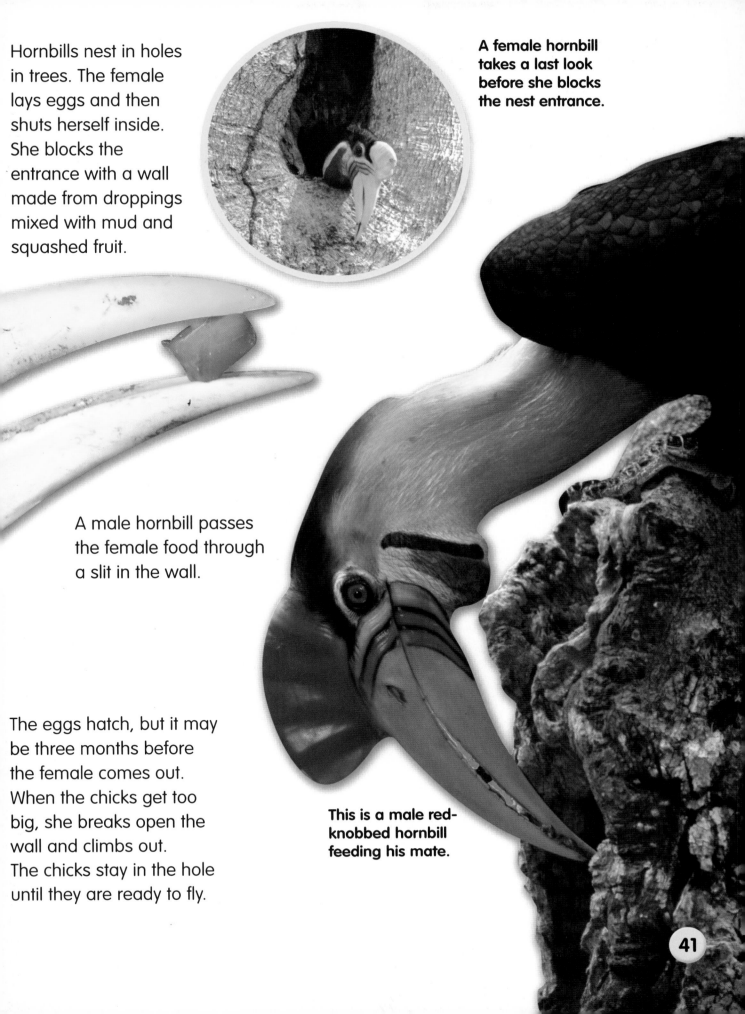

A female hornbill takes a last look before she blocks the nest entrance.

A male hornbill passes the female food through a slit in the wall.

The eggs hatch, but it may be three months before the female comes out. When the chicks get too big, she breaks open the wall and climbs out. The chicks stay in the hole until they are ready to fly.

This is a male red-knobbed hornbill feeding his mate.

41

Emperor penguins

Penguin pairs stay together for years.

Penguins cannot fly. They use their wings as flippers to swim in the ocean. Emperor penguin do not build nests. After mating, the female lays one egg. The male holds the egg on his feet to keep it warm.

This new chick is warm on Dad's fee!

The female leaves to catch fish. Sometimes emperor penguins walk for 60 mi. (100km) to get to the ocean.

All winter long, the male cares for the egg. In the spring, the egg hatches and the female returns with food for the chick.

LIFE CYCLE FACT
The female emperor penguin lays one egg. The chick hatches after around 65 days.

Big chicks stand in a huddle to protect themselves from the snow and icy winds.

When the egg has hatched, the male and female take turns caring for the chick and fishing.

Until its adult feathers grow, the chick cannot swim. After four or five months, the chick's feathers grow and it is able to go to find food on its own.

The parent penguin coughs up partially digested fish from its throat for the chick.

Arctic terns catch fish by plunging into the ocean.

Arctic terns

The arctic tern is the champion bird traveler. Each year, this small sea bird **migrates** from the Arctic to Antarctica and back again. Arctic terns fly around 22,000 mi. (35,000km) around the world every year.

Arctic terns have two summers every year.

When it is winter in the north of the world, it is summer in the south. Arctic terns fly south to escape the cold northern winter. When the southern summer ends, they fly north again.

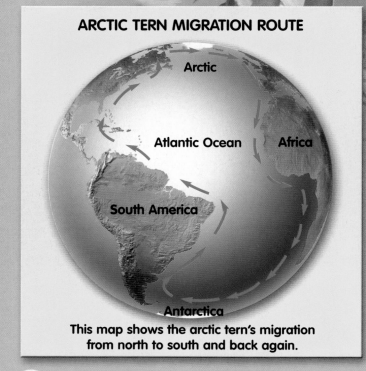

ARCTIC TERN MIGRATION ROUTE

Arctic

Atlantic Ocean

Africa

South America

Antarctica

This map shows the arctic tern's migration from north to south and back again.

Arctic terns pair for life. They mate and lay their eggs in the Arctic.

Chick

The parent terns raise their chicks during the short Arctic summer. When it's time to fly south, the parent terns guide the young to show them the way.

LIFE CYCLE FACT
The female arctic tern lays two or three eggs. The chicks hatch after around 24 days.

The parents bring the chicks fish to eat.

**The satin bowerbird
has blue-black feathers
and bright blue eyes.**

Bowerbirds

Bowerbirds live in Australia and New Guinea. The male builds a little archway, called a bower, to attract a mate. He puts colorful things, such as stones, bones, feathers, and shells, inside the bower. He makes a garden, too

The male dances in and out of his bower. Females visit several bowers before deciding on a mate.

LIFE CYCLE FACT
The female satin bowerbird lays two or three eggs. The chicks hatch after between 15 and 30 days.

Bower

Sometimes males steal decorations from one another's bowers!

This bird is taking a small blue block!

Satin bowerbirds like the color blue. A male may collect blue drinking straws, pieces of blue plastic, and even blue pens!

Male

Female

This is a pair of great bowerbirds.

After mating, the female bowerbird makes a saucer-shaped nest for her eggs. The male doesn't help—he is more interested in his bower.

Tailorbirds don't mind people. Some even nest in gardens.

Tailorbirds

The tailorbird lives in South Asia. It makes a very unusual nest. Just as a **tailor** sews cloth to make clothes, the tailorbird sews leaves together to make a nest.

First a tailorbird chooses a long, wide leaf. Using its beak as a needle, it sews the edges of the leaf together to make a bag shape.

Leaf

For thread, the bird uses plant fibers or a spider's web. It makes neat, tight stitches. Inside the leaf bag, the bird makes a cozy nest using a spider's web, pieces of string, or anything else soft.

Soft nest material

LIFE CYCLE FACT
The female tailorbird lays between three and five eggs. The chicks hatch after 12 days.

Stitches

This tailorbird nest has dried out. The chicks have left.

Leaf bag

The female sits on the eggs to incubate them. Both parents feed the chicks insects and spiders.

Puffins eat fish—they can carry ten small fish sideways in their beaks.

Puffins

The puffin is a sea bird that nests on cliffs. Puffins are excellent swimmers. Male and female puffins do a **courtship** dance—they bob heads and touch beaks. Then they mate out at sea.

The puffin pair digs a nest burrow, using their beaks and feet. Some puffins nest inside empty rabbit holes.

A courtship dance

LIFE CYCLE FACT
The female puffin lays one egg. The chick hatches after around 40 days.

Burrow entrance

Inside the burrow, the female lays one egg. Both parents incubate the egg and catch fish for the chick when it hatches.

When the chick is six weeks old, the parents leave it. After a week on its own, the chick leaves the burrow.

Nest material

Puffin chick

The chick rushes to the ocean, usually at night, when there are few predators around. Rats and seagulls kill puffin chicks.

That's amazing!

Birds are very good parents. They care for their eggs and chicks by building safe, cozy homes and bringing them food. But did you know that there is one bird that's a very lazy parent?

Swallows stick their nests onto houses or cave walls, using their gummy saliva as glue.

The cuckoo lays its egg in the nest of another bird and then leaves it. The other bird does not notice the strange egg. The cuckoo chick hatches after 12 days and pushes the other eggs or chicks out of the nest.

The cuckoo gets all the food and is soon bigger than its new parents.

Cuckoo chick

Wagtail adult

Nest

Ostrich egg

Chicken egg

African weaverbirds nest in **colonies**. Each pair of birds weaves a nest from grass and leaves.

An ostrich egg is the biggest egg in the bird kingdom. A hummingbird's egg is the smallest—it's around the size of a pea!

AMAZING BIRD FACT
Ostrich chicks are cared for by their dad—Mom doesn't help at all!

Fish Families

What is a fish?

Fish are covered in scales that help protect them.

A fish is an animal that lives in water. A fish usually has fins and scales. It can breathe under the water using body parts called **gills**. The gills take **oxygen** out of the water and pass it into the fish's body.

Fish use their fins and tail to move through the water.

Fin

Gill cover

Some fish live alone. Others live in big groups called **schools**. A school can have hundreds or thousands of fish.

Fin

These fish eggs have been attached to an underwater rock by a female fish.

Most fish **reproduce** by laying eggs. The eggs are very small and soft. A female fish usually lays hundreds of eggs at one time.

Sharks are a type of fish. Some sharks, such as the great white shark, give birth to live babies called pups.

A great white shark

Tail

AMAZING FISH FACT
When great white shark pups are born, they are more than 3 ft. (1m) long and have sharp teeth, ready for hunting!

57

Mom meets Dad

This is a pair of long-nosed butterfly fish. All butterfly fish pair for life.

Most fish reproduce every year. Some fish find a mate and stay together as a pair for life. Other fish have a new partner each year. Many fish mate with more than one partner in the same year.

Hammerhead sharks can live in schools of more than 500 sharks. The strongest female swims in the middle of the school.

When she is ready to mate the strongest female starts shaking her head from side to side. This makes the other females swim to the edge of the school.

AMAZING FISH FACT

Sharks live in every ocean of the world. They have been around since before the dinosaurs!

Now the strongest female is the center of attention and is sure to get a mate.

Freshwater angelfish stay together as a pair for life. After mating, the female lays around 1,000 eggs on a leaf.

Eggs

A male emperor angelfish lives with up to five female mates. If the male dies, one of the females turns into a male fish and becomes the leader of the group!

Emperor angelfish live in coral reefs.

59

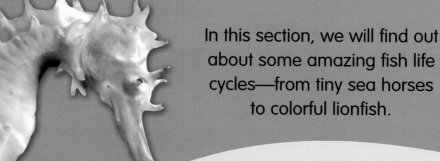

In this section, we will find out about some amazing fish life cycles—from tiny sea horses to colorful lionfish.

Sea horse

Lionfish

Amazing fish life cycles

1 A pair of lionfish

An adult male and female fish meet. Some fish make a nest.

FISH LIFE CYCLE
Many fish have a life cycle with these stages.

2 Fertilized fish eggs

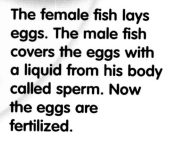

The female fish lays eggs. The male fish covers the eggs with a liquid from his body called sperm. Now the eggs are fertilized.

4 Baby salmon

Baby fish, called fry, hatch from the eggs. The tiny babies take care of themselves. They have a yolk sac that they use as food.

3 A pair of angelfish

Some fish guard their eggs. Others leave them to hatch on their own.

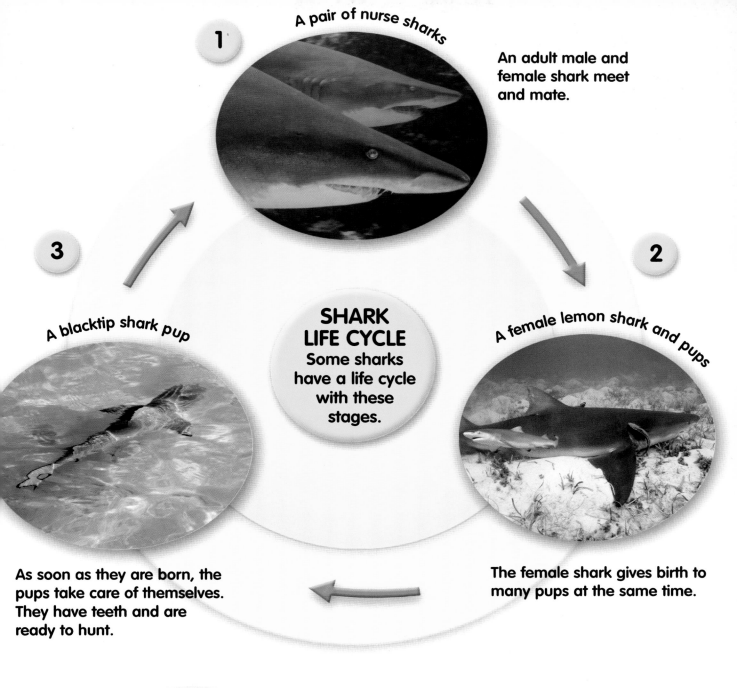

1 A pair of nurse sharks

An adult male and female shark meet and mate.

SHARK LIFE CYCLE
Some sharks have a life cycle with these stages.

2 A female lemon shark and pups

The female shark gives birth to many pups at the same time.

3 A blacktip shark pup

As soon as they are born, the pups take care of themselves. They have teeth and are ready to hunt.

AMAZING FISH FACT

This is a pair of red flowerhorn fish. There are around 24,500 different types of fish.

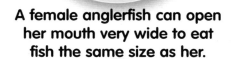

Deep-sea anglerfish

Anglerfish live at the bottom of deep oceans where it is very dark. The female has a long spine that sticks out of her head. On the end is a ball that can glow like a light.

A female anglerfish can open her mouth very wide to eat fish the same size as her.

The female anglerfish uses her light to attract other fish—then she eats them!

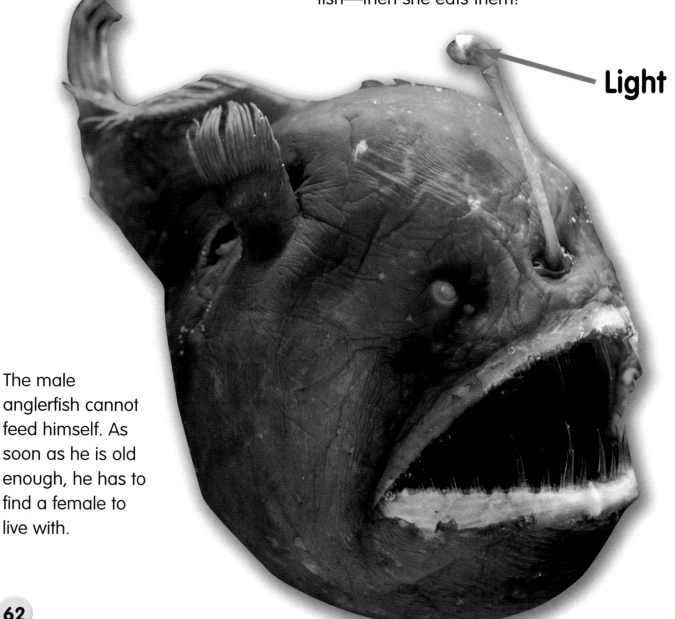

Light

The male anglerfish cannot feed himself. As soon as he is old enough, he has to find a female to live with.

The small male attaches himself to a female. They stay together for life. The male gets smaller and smaller.

Female

Male

When it is time to reproduce and lay eggs, the female already has her mate with her.

Salmon

Adult salmon live in the oceans. In the fall, whe
it is time to mate and lay eggs, they have to sw
back to the freshwater river where they were bo

**A salmon who is ready to
reproduce is called a spawner.**

The salmon have a dangerou
journey. They have to swim a
long way and must swim
upstream, which is very tiring

AMAZING FISH FACT

The salmon have to leap
up waterfalls and avoid
predators such as
grizzly bears.

Grizzly bears

Salmon

When a female salmon reaches the spawning ground, she makes four or five nests called redds. She lays around 1,000 eggs in each nest. Then a male fertilizes the eggs.

Thousands of spawners gather in the same place.

The eggs hatch after four months. The small salmon are called alevins. They have an orange yolk sac that contains all the food they need to grow.

The young salmon grow bigger and bigger. After around three years, they are ready to swim out to sea.

Alevin

Yolk sac

Sticklebacks feed on tiny shellfish and the fry and eggs of other fish.

Sticklebacks

Sticklebacks are tiny fish—they grow to only 2 in. (5cm) long. Some sticklebacks live in **salt water** close to the **coast**. Others live in freshwater ponds, lakes, and rivers.

Nest

Between March and August, the male stickleback changes color to attract a mate.

Then the male stickleback builds a nest from plant pieces. He does a zigzag dance in front of the nest to attract a female.

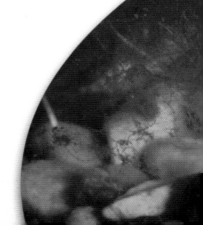

During the mating season, the underside of the male's body becomes a bright orange-red color, his eyes turn blue, and silver scales appear on his back.

Many different females lay their eggs in the male's nest. Then he fertilizes them.

AMAZING FISH FACT
The male stickleback guards the eggs in his nest and cares for the young after they hatch.

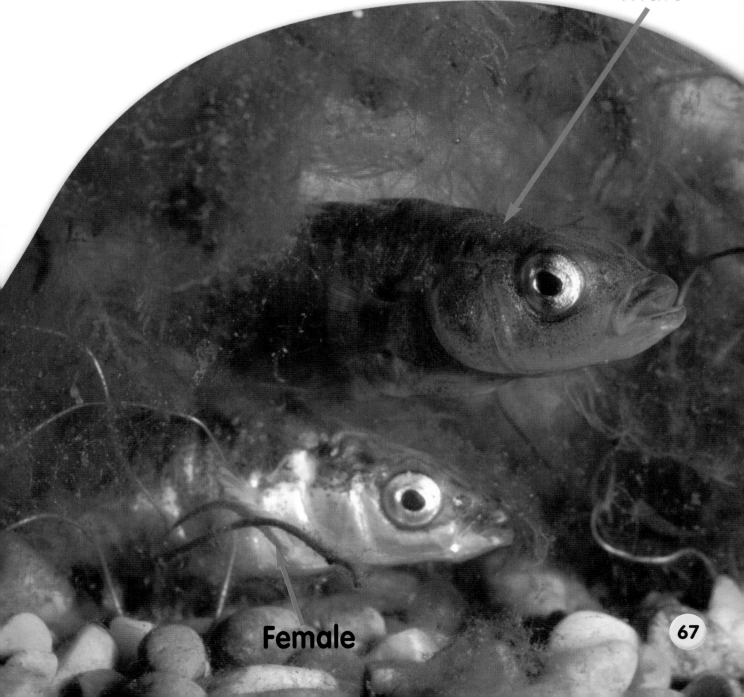

Male

Female

Sea horses

This very unusual-looking fish has a horselike head and a tail that it uses to hold onto things. The sea horse can move each of its eyes separately—one can look forward while the other looks backward.

The sea horse's body is covered in armor made of hard, bony sections.

Before they mate, the male and female sea horses hold each other's tails, swim side by side, or swing around together on a piece of seaweed.

Most types of sea horses pair for life.

The male sea horse has a pouch on his stomach. The pouch is like a pocket. The female lays eggs inside the pouch and the male sea horse carries the eggs.

When the babies hatch, the male gives birth. He holds onto a piece of seaweed with his long tail. He rocks back and forth until the babies pop out of his pouch. This can last for around two days.

**Baby
sea horses**

Pouch

**AMAZING
FISH FACT**
Sea horses can change color to match their surroundings.

Reptile and Amphibian Families

What is a reptile?

This is a crocodile's foot—you can see its scaly skin.

A reptile is an animal with a thick skin covered in scales. Reptiles are **ectothermic**. This means that their body temperature goes up or down with the temperature of the air or water around them.

Snakes, lizards, crocodiles, alligators, tortoises, and turtles are all reptiles.

Snakes are reptiles with no legs.

Scales

Every few months, a snake wiggles out of its old skin. A shiny new skin, one size bigger, has grown underneath.

Old skin

Lizards are reptiles. Most lizards have four legs and a tail.

If a predator, such as a bird, grabs a lizard's tail, the tip breaks off. The bird is left with the twitching tail. The lizard runs away and soon grows a new tail!

AMAZING REPTILE FACT

Giant Galápagos tortoises can live to be more than 100 years old!

This agama lizard is growing a new tail—the tip is missing.

Tortoises and turtles are reptiles with shells.

A giant Galápagos tortoise

73

Reptile life

Adult reptiles usually live on their own. Males and females get together to mate and then separate again. After mating, most female reptiles lay eggs, but some give birth to live babies.

This emerald tree boa gives birth to live babies.

Chameleons are tree lizards that can change their skin color. A female shows a male that she is ready to mate by changing color.

AMAZING REPTILE FACT
Reptile eggs feel rubbery. The shells are softer than a bird's egg, but strong.

A pair of chameleons

Reptiles lay many eggs at one time. Only a few hatch—the rest are often eaten by other animals.

Female

Male

Female pythons coil their bodies around their eggs to keep them warm.

Most reptile mothers leave their eggs to hatch on their own, but some look after their eggs.

When a baby reptile hatches, it looks like a tiny copy of its parents. The baby is ready to find its own food right away. Baby snakes can hunt as soon as they are born.

Egg

This western pond turtle has just hatched.

75

What is an amphibian?

An amphibian is an animal that lives in both water and on land. Like reptiles, amphibians are ectothermic. Their bodies are the same temperature as the air or water around them. Amphibians have smooth skin.

This is a toad. It looks like a frog, but it has drier, bumpier skin.

Frogs, toads, newts, salamanders, and caecilians are all amphibians.

This is a caecilian. It has no legs and looks like a snake.

Newts and salamanders are amphibians with tails.

This is a fire salamander.

Most amphibians like warm, damp places with plenty of plants that they can use as hiding places.

Frogs and toads are amphibians with no tails.

The bright blue color of this poison-arrow frog tells predators, "Stay away—I'm poisonous."

Amphibian life

Amphibian eggs have no shells. A frog's eggs look like jelly.

Adult amphibians usually live on their own. Males and females get together to mate. After mating, female amphibians lay eggs. Most amphibians lay their eggs in water. This stops the eggs from drying out.

In the spring, male and female frogs and toads go to ponds to mate. Then the females lay eggs.

AMAZING AMPHIBIAN FACT
Male frogs puff out their throats to sing a croaky song. This attracts females.

Baby amphibians hatch from eggs. They have large heads, long tails, and breathe through gills, like fish. Soon they grow legs and begin breathing with lungs. Then they can live on land.

These are the young of a spotted salamander.

Eggs

Most amphibians don't take care of their eggs or babies, but there are some amazing amphibian parents.

Some poison-arrow frogs lay their eggs in water-filled hollows in trees. They carry the tadpoles to a new home if the water dries out.

A male midwife toad carries his eggs on his back until they hatch.

Komodo dragon

In this section, we will find out about some amazing reptile and amphibian life cycles—from the giant Komodo dragon to the tiny red-eyed tree frog.

Red-eyed tree frog

Amazing reptile and amphibian life cycles

1 A pair of rattlesnakes

A male and female snake meet and mate.

4 A young emerald tree boa

SNAKE LIFE CYCLE
All reptiles have a life cycle with these stages.

2 A female corn snake

The baby snakes are ready to go off on their own as soon as they hatch or are born.

3 A baby ball python

The female lays eggs. Some snakes give birth to live babies.

Baby snakes hatch from the eggs.

A male and female frog meet and mate.

1

The baby frogs leave the water. They grow bigger and bigger.

5

The female lays hundreds of eggs in the water.

2

FROG LIFE CYCLE
Most amphibians have a life cycle with these stages.

3

4

Over several weeks, the tadpoles grow legs, and lungs for breathing air on land. They lose their tails.

Tadpoles with tails hatch from the eggs. They swim in the water and breathe through gills, like fish.

AMAZING REPTILE FACT

This male Jackson's chameleon uses his **horns** to fight other males for females.

**A crocodile can bite,
but it cannot chew.**

Nile crocodiles

Nile crocodiles live beside lakes and rivers in Africa. They wait for big animals, such as antelope, to come for a drink, and then they grab them to eat! Nile crocodiles also eat monkeys, turtles, birds, and fish.

After she has mated, a female crocodile makes a nest beside a river. She lays between 50 and 60 eggs.

After around 60 days, the eggs hatch.

Baby crocodile

AMAZING REPTILE FACT
A male Nile crocodile can grow up to 20 ft. (6m) long.

Crocodiles are fierce, but they are very good mothers. They guard their eggs and even help break them open with their mouths so that the babies can get out.

The baby crocodiles call to their mother to let her know they are hatching.

The female looks after the babies in the shallow water of a river. After around eight weeks, the babies go off on their own.

The female gently carries the babies in her mouth from the nest to the river.

Green turtles

The green turtle lives in warm oceans. Green turtles eat underwater plants such as sea grass. Female green turtles travel to the same beach every year to mate and lay eggs.

An adult green turtle can weigh 440 lbs. (220kg).

AMAZING REPTILE FACT

Some females swim around 600 mi. (1,000km) to get to their breeding beach. It can take weeks!

Turtles swim by paddling with their flippers.

The adult male and female turtles meet and mate in shallow water.

Flipper

The green turtle lays up to 200 eggs.

The female turtle digs a deep hole in the sand with her flippers. She lays her eggs, covers them with sand, and then crawls back to the sea.

The baby turtles hatch after around seven weeks. The babies have to take care of themselves. They dig out of the sand and dash to the water.

The tiny turtle hatchlings are in danger of being eaten by predators such as sea birds.

The dragon's saliva is so full of germs that just one bite can kill its prey.

Komodo dragons

The Komodo dragon is the world's largest lizard. This giant reptile lives on Komodo island in Indonesia and two other islands in Southeast Asia. Komodo dragons hunt for wild pigs and deer. They also eat animals that are already dead.

Male Komodos stand on their back legs to wrestle in order to attract a mate.

An adult male can be 10 ft. (3m) long!

After mating, the female scrapes out a shallow nest in the ground and lays around 25 eggs. She then leaves the eggs to hatch on their own.

The dragon's eggs hatch after between seven and nine months. The babies climb trees and eat insects and lizards. Trees are safe, because if an adult dragon catches a baby, it will eat it!

This baby dragon is two days old and around 12 in. (30cm) long.

AMAZING REPTILE FACT

A female Komodo dragon in a British zoo laid eggs that hatched into babies even though she had no male around to mate with!

**AMAZING AMPHIBIAN
LIFE CYCLE**

**The frog's toes have
suction pads to help
it stick to leaves.**

The red-eyed tree frog lives in **rainforests** in Central America. It is a nocturnal frog. This means it rests during the day and is active at night. Red-eyed tree frogs eat insects.

During the breeding season, male red-eyed tree frogs gather together on branches over a pond.

**AMAZING
AMPHIBIAN FACT**

With its eyes closed, the frog blends into its green habitat. If attacked, it opens its big red eyes—this startles predators.

The males call to females with a clicking noise.

After mating, the female lays up to 50 eggs on a leaf that hangs over the pond. Laying many eggs at one time means at least some babies will survive.

After around five days, the eggs hatch and the tadpoles fall down into the pond below.

Tadpole

When these tadpoles have grown into frogs, they will climb back up trees.

89

Darwin's frogs

The Darwin's frog lives near rivers in damp, shady mountain forests in South America. Darwin's frogs eat insects and small animals such as worms. The males are very good father

This frog has an unusual pointed, wobbly section on the end of its nose!

When a female Darwin's frog has laid her eggs, the male guards them. After around two weeks, the babies inside the eggs start to move. Then the male picks up the eggs with his tongue and puts them inside his mouth.

The eggs are in here!

The male puts up to 15 eggs into a pouch inside his mouth.

The tadpoles hatch inside the male's mouth. They stay in his mouth for 50 days, feeding on their egg yolks. When they have grown into little froglets, the babies climb out of Dad's mouth.

An adult Darwin's frog is less than one inch long!

Froglet

That's amazing!

Are you ready for some more amazing reptile and amphibian facts? Did you know there's a toad that doesn't have tadpoles, a snake that's as long as six men, and a lizard that's left over from prehistoric times?

The North American bullfrog lays 25,000 eggs at one time!

These men are carrying an anaconda.

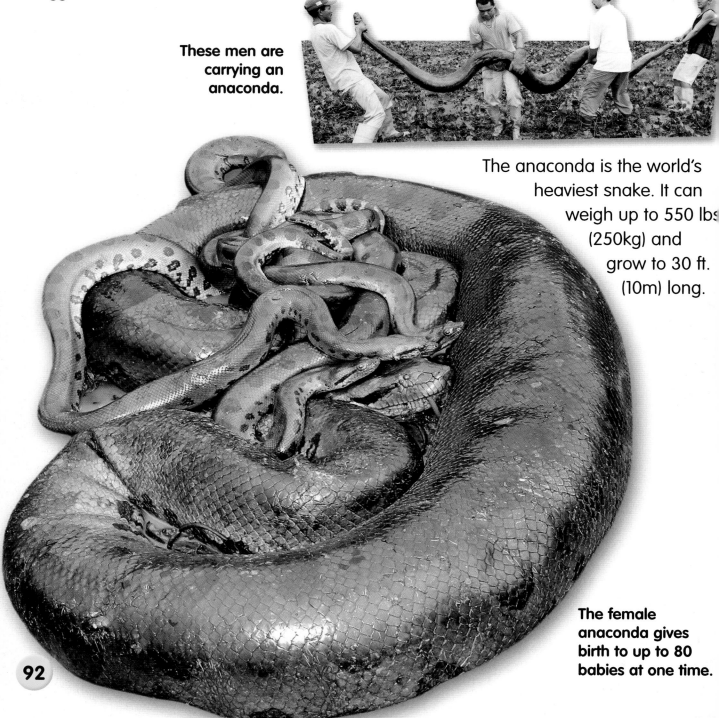

The anaconda is the world's heaviest snake. It can weigh up to 550 lbs (250kg) and grow to 30 ft. (10m) long.

The female anaconda gives birth to up to 80 babies at one time.

There are no tadpoles in the Suriname toad's life cycle.

The female Suriname toad lays eggs and the male puts them onto her back. A protective covering of skin grows over the eggs. When the eggs hatch, baby toads break through the skin.

Eggs and baby toads

The tuatara is in a reptile family all of its own. Its closest relatives lived in prehistoric times, among the dinosaurs.

AMAZING REPTILE FACT
When resting, tuataras may take only one breath per hour!

Baby tuataras do not hatch from their eggs for 12–15 months— the longest time for any reptile.

Glossary

amphibians—cold-blooded animals that lay their eggs in water but live on land as adults.

ancestors—parents, grandparents, great-grandparents—all the earlier relatives who came before you.

breed—to mate and have babies.

burrows—tunnels and holes under the ground where some animals live.

coast—the land along a seashore and the area around it.

colonies—large groups of animals.

coral reefs—underwater places that look rocky but are actually made from the bodies of coral animals called polyps. The polyps have hard skeletons that join together. When a polyp dies, its skeleton stays as part of the reef, so the reef gets bigger and bigger.

courtship—trying to win a mate.

den—a wild animal's home.

digested—when food is broken down in the stomach into materials that the body can then use to provide energy.

down—a bird's soft, fine feathers.

ectothermic—an ectothermic animal needs sunshine to warm up and become active.

endothermic—describes animals whose body temperature stays the same no matter how hot or cold the air or water is around them. You are endothermic!

fertilized—when an egg is made to develop into a young animal.

flippers—flat limbs that some animals use to help them swim. Flippers don't have fingers, so an animal can move easily through the water. Seals and turtles have flippers.

fresh water—water without salt in it. Most lakes have fresh water.

gills—breathing organs (parts of the body) in animals that live in water.

grasslands—wide, open grassy spaces with few trees.

hatch—when a baby bird or animal breaks out of its egg.

herd—a group of animals that lives together.

hollow—something that is empty inside.

horns—bony growths that are found on top of some animals' heads. Horns can be used for fighting off other animals.

hunting—going out to look for prey to eat.

incubation—keeping an egg warm after laying, before it hatches.

mammals—endothermic animals with hair that feed their babies milk.

marsupials—animals that have a pouch on the front of the body in which they carry their babies. Kangaroos and koalas are marsupials.

mate—when a male and female animal meet and have babies.

migrates—travels a long way to find food or a place to breed.

oxygen—a gas that all animals need in order to survive.

pouch—the pocketlike part on the front of a marsupial where the baby animal is carried.

predators—animals that hunt and kill other animals for food.

prehistoric—a long time ago, before written records.

prey—animals that are hunted by other animals for food.

rainforests—forests of tall trees in areas with a lot of rain.

reproduce—to have babies.

reptiles—animals with scales such as snakes, lizards, and crocodiles.

salt water—water with salt in it. The oceans have salt water.

scales—small, overlapping sections of hard skin that cover fish and reptiles.

schools—groups of fish that swim together.

stages—different times of an animal's life when the animal changes.

suckling—feeding on mother's milk.

tailor—someone who makes clothes.

temperature—how hot or cold something is.

territory—an area or place where an animal feeds and breeds.

tusks—long, sharp pointed teeth.

upstream—the opposite direction to the flow of water in a river or stream.

Index